EDGE BOOKS™

WARRIORS OF HISTORY

COMANCHE WARRIORS

by Mary Englar

j355.02089
ENGLAR

Consultant:
Professor Troy Johnson
American Indian Studies,
California State University,
Long Beach, California

Capstone
press®

Mankato, Minnesota

Edge Books are published by Capstone Press,
151 Good Counsel Drive, P.O. Box 669, Mankato, Minnesota 56002.
www.capstonepress.com

Library of Congress Cataloging-in-Publication Data
Englar, Mary.
    Comanche warriors / by Mary Englar.
    p. cm. — (Edge books. Warriors of history)
    Includes bibliographical references and index.
    ISBN-13: 978-1-4296-1311-8 (hardcover)
    ISBN-10: 1-4296-1311-4 (hardcover)
    1. Comanche Indians — Wars. 2. Indian weapons — Great Plains. 3. Comanche
Indians — History. 4. Comanche Indians — Government relations. I. Title. II. Series.
E99.C85E65 2008
355.02089'974572 — dc22   2007029960

Summary: Describes the life of a Comanche warrior, including his training, weapons,
    and what led to the downfall of his society.

Editorial Credits

Mandy Robbins, editor; Thomas Emery, set designer; Kyle Grenz, book designer;
    Jo Miller, photo researcher; Tod Smith, illustrator; Krista Ward, colorist

Photo Credits

Alamy/Chuck Place, 28–29; Frymire Archive, 9; INTERFOTO Pressbildagentur, 12
Corbis, cover, 27; Bettmann, 16
Getty Images Inc./Hulton Archives, 22
North Wind Picture Archives, 4, 6–7, 10, 14–15, 19, 24

1 2 3 4 5 6 13 12 11 10 09 08

TABLE OF CONTENTS

CHAPTER 1
THE GREAT PLAINS

The Comanche used every part of the buffalo for food, cloth, tools, or weapons.

Before Europeans came to North America, there were no bustling cities, no highways, and no cars or trains. North America was a beautiful, unspoiled wilderness. At that time, hundreds of thousands of American Indians called this land home. Many Indian nations hunted buffalo on the Great Plains. This area stretched across the center of the continent from Canada to Mexico.

The Comanche Indians lived in family groups that hunted together. Around 1700, small bands of Comanche left the Rocky Mountains. They traveled to the grassy plains to be closer to the buffalo herds.

Buffalo provided nearly everything the Comanche needed. Women made clothing and shelters from the hides. After the Comanche ate the fresh meat, the women dried the rest for winter. Men used bones to make tools. They also used tissue called sinew to string their bows.

The Comanche didn't want to share their valuable hunting grounds. As the Comanche moved onto the plains, they fought the Cheyenne, Crow, Pawnee, and Sioux for hunting grounds. The wars forced the Comanche to move to what is now the state of Texas.

Buffalo were as important to the Comanche as air and water. They were willing to give their lives fighting for hunting grounds.

DISCOVERING HORSES

The Comanche had never seen horses until the early 1600s. Spanish colonists brought horses to their North American colonies in 1598. Eventually, many horses escaped into the wilderness. Indian tribes captured these horses, bred them, and traded them.

By the 1800s, the Comanche were the most skilled warriors on horseback. The Comanche rode horses during hunts and battles.

If they could not trade for horses, the Comanche raided ranches and Indian camps. They attacked at dawn, waking up their enemies. Comanche warriors attacked with bows or guns from a distance. The speed of the Comanche horses made the warriors difficult to shoot.

The Comanches preferred pinto horses. They believed the pintos' spotted color gave the horses sacred power.

CHAPTER II

WARRIORS ON HORSEBACK

LEARN ABOUT:

- Warriors from birth
- Training for battle
- Test of manhood

Comanche boys learned to train
and ride horses at a young age.

To the Comanche, horses were like money. They traded horses for guns and supplies. Young warriors raided for horses to earn respect. When young men wanted to marry, they gave the bride's father a gift of horses. Giving his finest horses showed how much a young man valued his future wife.

Neighboring Indian nations often attacked Comanche camps to steal their huge herds of horses. As a result, Comanche warriors were always prepared for an attack. Raiders could kill men and capture women and children. Comanche men fought hard to protect their family members and their horses.

For Comanche men, brave acts earned them respect from their families and other warriors. Saving another Comanche warrior during battle was considered a brave act. Hand-to-hand combat was rare, but it earned warriors the greatest respect and celebration.

White settlers killed many of the buffalo in Comanche territory. The Comanche were forced to raid wagon trains to get food and tools once supplied by buffalo.

WARRIOR TRAINING

Warriors were the most important members of the band. Every Comanche boy wanted to be a warrior, and every man was needed to protect the band. Comanche boys learned about the warrior's role at a young age.

Around age 5, many boys got their first horses. Boys rode every day to learn how to handle the horses. Older boys practiced picking heavy objects off the ground while galloping. Eventually, they could pick up a man. This skill helped them save fellow warriors during battle.

Teenage boys rode along on hunts. They learned to kill buffalo in a full-speed chase. A boy had to make his first hunting kill before he could go to war.

The final test of manhood for young men was to ride on their first raid. To earn respect, young men had to kill enemies and capture horses for their band.

EDGE FACT

Comanche fathers often hung tiny hunting bows on their sons' cradleboards. As a boy grew, his father made him larger and larger bows.

HORSE TRAINING

A Comanche warrior's most prized possessions were his horses. Most warriors kept several horses for hunts and battles.

Warriors trained their horses for hunting as well as war. A warrior pressed his knees into the horse to direct it to the left or right. Horses learned to gallop fearlessly alongside buffalo. Once the hunter shot an arrow, the horse turned away to avoid the wounded buffalo.

Comanche warriors rode on the side of their horses. The horses shielded the warriors from their enemies.

In battle, Comanche warriors often surrounded their enemies. Many warriors slid down on to one side of their horses. A warrior hooked one foot over the horse's back and shot arrows from under the horse's neck. The horse's body protected a warrior from being killed or wounded.

CHAPTER III
WEAPONS OF WAR

Taking enemy scalps proved a warrior's success in battle. The Comanche believed a scalped enemy could not enter the spirit world.

The Comanche's most important weapons were their bows and arrows. Bows were about 4 feet (1.2 meters) long. Warriors preferred bows made from Osage orange trees. The wood was strong and flexible.

War arrows had jagged tips to make them more deadly. When enemies tried to pull out the arrow, the jagged edges tore through their flesh. Comanche were so skilled with their bows that they often used them instead of guns. Warriors could fire a dozen arrows in the time it took to reload a gun.

WAR PARTIES

Each band had a war chief. The war chief was a highly respected warrior. War chiefs called all the band's men to a council before going to war. The war chief convinced them that he had sacred power. The Comanche believed that the war chief's power would make their raids successful.

War parties raided ranches or Indian camps for horses. They also raided to get revenge for an earlier loss of people or horses. Comanche warriors sometimes rode hundreds of miles on raids.

Successful raids depended on surprise. If the Comanche could not surprise the enemy, they often returned to their camp. They could raid for horses any time. But they could not replace their bravest and most skilled warriors.

A war chief couldn't plan an attack without the support of the other men in his band.

Lance
In the 1740s, French traders brought steel to the Comanche. Warriors used steel to make lance points instead of using traditional stone or bones.

Bow
Comanche bows were powerful enough to drive an arrow completely through a buffalo.

Shield
Comanche warriors often decorated their shields with scalps they had taken.

SACRED POWER

Comanche warriors prepared for war by painting black stripes across their foreheads and faces. They also painted their bodies and their horses. They believed this artwork gave them sacred power. It also frightened their enemies.

Some warriors wore headdresses made from buffalo skulls. A headdress included buffalo horns and a flap of furry hide.

Buffalo hide shields represented a warrior's bravery. Warriors decorated their shields with bear teeth, horsehair, and human hair. The decorations represented their belief in their sacred power over animals and enemies.

CHAPTER IV

PROUD PEOPLE SURRENDER

LEARN ABOUT:

- American invasion
- Forced onto reservations
- Quanah Parker's last stand

White travelers killed buffalo for sport and left their bodies to rot.

In 1848, people discovered gold in California. Thousands of Americans followed the Santa Fe Trail across Comanche territory. The travelers killed thousands of buffalo for sport, taking away much of the Comanche's food supply. They also brought strange new diseases. Smallpox and cholera killed almost half of the Comanche by the late 1800s.

TREATY OF MEDICINE LODGE

In 1867, U.S. government officials decided that all Plains Indians should move to reservations. General William T. Sherman spoke to 4,000 American Indians at Medicine Lodge Creek in Kansas. The group included Comanche, Kiowa, Cheyenne, and Arapaho Indians. Sherman told the chiefs that they had to settle on reservations in Indian Territory. The U.S. government promised the Indians schools, farming supplies, and houses if they signed a treaty agreeing to move.

After the Treaty of Medicine Lodge, thousands of American Indians made the difficult journey to reservations.

By signing the treaty, the Comanche agreed to give up their last buffalo hunting grounds in Texas. They also promised to stop raiding American settlements. But the chiefs who signed the treaty did not represent all of the Comanche. Many Comanche weren't at the treaty council and never agreed to give up their land.

CYNTHIA ANN PARKER

Many Plains Indians captured enemy women and children. Some were adopted into the tribe or traded to other tribes. Others were sold to the Spanish as slaves.

Many American children captured by the Comanche grew up as members of the band. When recaptured by the Americans, they often wanted to return to their Indian families.

In 1836, Comanche Indians captured nine-year-old Cynthia Ann Parker from her family's home in Texas. She was adopted into the Comanche tribe and later married a chief named Peta Nocona. He was killed by the Texas Rangers in 1860. The Rangers returned Cynthia to Austin, Texas. She wanted to return to her Indian family, but her white family never allowed it. Cynthia Ann died in 1870. She was the mother of Chief Quanah Parker.

THE LAST FREE COMANCHE

The Comanche who didn't sign the Medicine Lodge Treaty continued hunting buffalo and raiding ranches. They raided settlements in Texas. Then they retreated to camps hidden in the rocky canyons of the Texas Panhandle.

In 1874, Comanche Chief Quanah Parker's band joined other local Indians. They planned one of the last Indian raids. They wanted to attack a group of buffalo hunters staying at an old fort. Several hundred warriors joined the war party.

Two hunters were outside the fort at dawn. They saw the warriors and raised the alarm. Twenty-eight buffalo hunters held off hundreds of warriors. The hunters' powerful rifles could hit a warrior up to a mile away. Chief Parker's men did not want to lose many warriors, so they retreated. The chief led his band back to their camp in Palo Duro Canyon.

Chief Quanah Parker was a fearless leader. He was greatly respected by his fellow warriors.

The Comanche Homecoming celebration is held every summer in Oklahoma.

In September 1874, U.S. troops hunted down the last Comanche living off the reservations. The soldiers burned tepees, captured horses, and destroyed food and weapons. By December, most Indians had surrendered. Without horses and weapons, Chief Parker's band couldn't hunt for food. In June 1875, Parker and his band surrendered.

EDGE FACT

In 1835, Texans started a Corps of Rangers to fight Indians along the Texas frontier. These early fighters became the famous Texas Rangers.

THE TRADITION CONTINUES

The Comanche still honor and respect their warriors. Each year, the modern Comanche Nation holds a celebration called the Comanche Homecoming. It honors Comanche soldiers who fought in wars.

GLOSSARY

band (BAND) — a group of American Indians who are related to each other; a band is smaller than a tribe.

council (KAUN-suhl) — a meeting of a group of leaders chosen to look after the interests of a community

raid (RAYD) — a sudden, surprise attack on a place

reservation (rez-er-VAY-shuhn) — an area of land set aside by the U.S. government for American Indians

revenge (rih-VENJ) — an action taken to hurt someone who has hurt you or someone you care about

sacred (SAY-krid) — holy or having to do with religion

sinew (SIN-yoo) — a strong piece of body tissue that connects muscle to bone; Comanche warriors used sinew to string their bows.

surrender (suh-REN-dur) — to give up or admit defeat

treaty (TREE-tee) — an official agreement between two or more groups or countries

READ MORE

De Capua, Sarah. *The Comanche.* First Americans. New York: Marshall Cavendish Benchmark, 2007.

Knudsen, Shannon. *Quanah Parker.* History Maker Bios. Minneapolis: Lerner, 2004.

Yacowitz, Caryn. *Comanche Indians.* Native Americans. Chicago: Heinemann, 2003.

Zappler, Georg. *Learn About — Texas Indians.* Learn About Texas. Austin, Texas: University of Texas Press, 2007.

INTERNET SITES

FactHound offers a safe, fun way to find Internet sites related to this book. All of the sites on FactHound have been researched by our staff.

Here's how:
1. Visit *www.facthound.com*
2. Choose your grade level.
3. Type in this book ID **1429613114** for age-appropriate sites. You may also browse subjects by clicking on letters, or by clicking on pictures and words.
4. Click on the **Fetch It** button.

FactHound will fetch the best sites for you!

INDEX